THIS WALKER BOOK BELONGS TO:

DUDLEY SCHOOLS LIBRARY
AND INFORMATION SERVICE

D0336022

Schools Library and Information Services
S00000666751

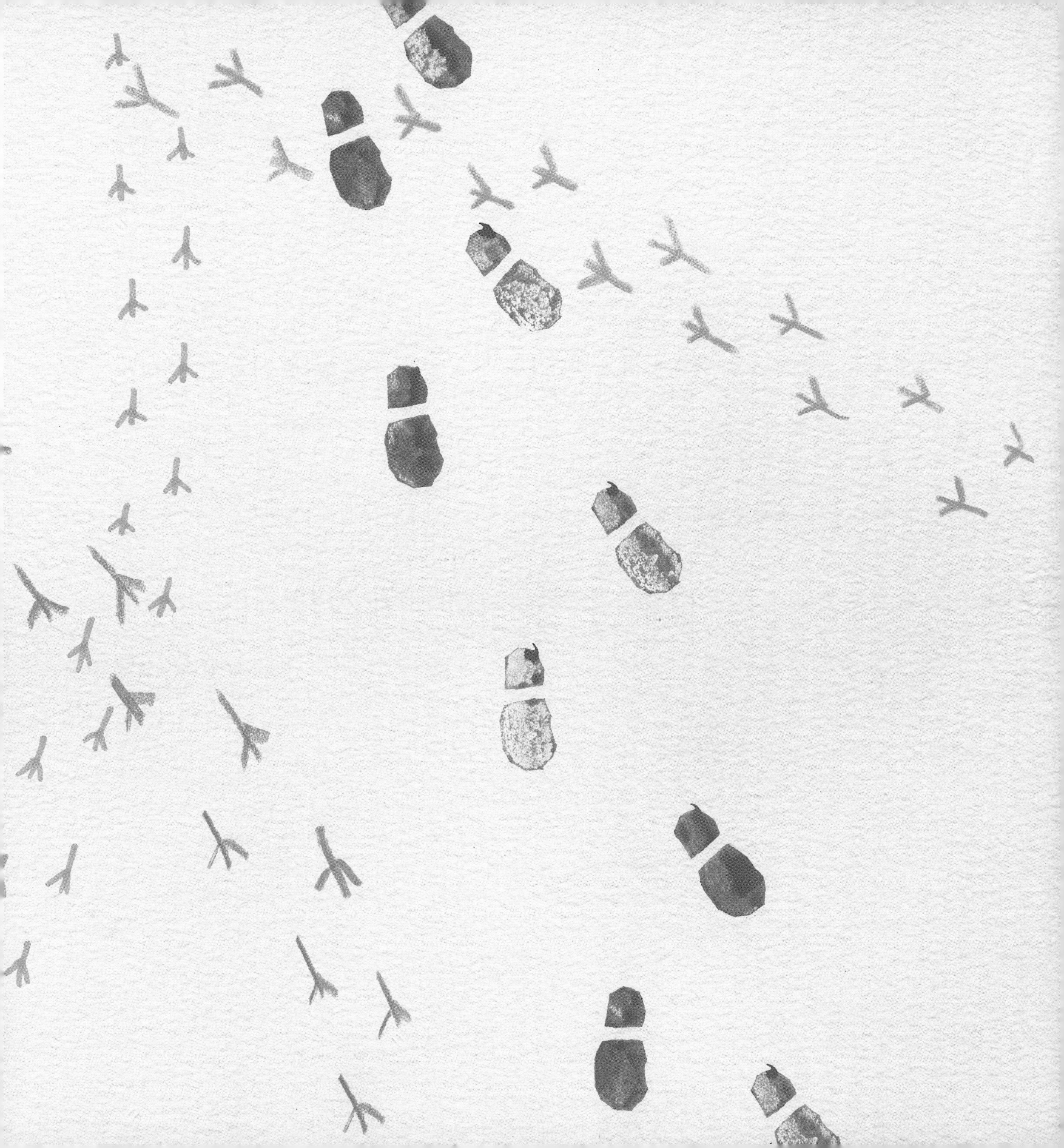

For Kate Smith

DUDLEY PUBLIC LIBRARIES
L 47922
666751 | | SCH
| JY DUN

First published 2004 by Walker Books Ltd
87 Vauxhall Walk, London SE11 5HJ

This edition published 2005

10 9 8 7 6 5 4 3 2 1

© 2004 Polly Dunbar

The right of Polly Dunbar to be identified as author/illustrator of this work has been asserted by her in accordance with the Copyright, Designs and Patents Act 1988

This book has been typeset in Colwell Roman

Printed in China All rights reserved

British Library Cataloguing in Publication Data:
a catalogue record for this book is available from the British Library

ISBN 1-84428-517-0

www.walkerbooks.co.uk

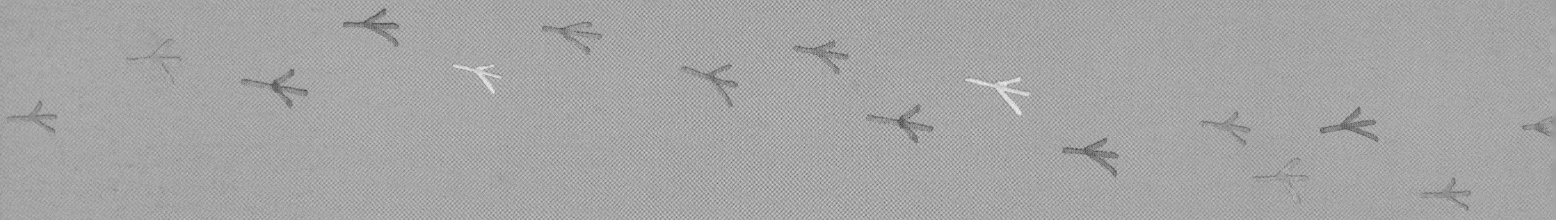

WALKER BOOKS
AND SUBSIDIARIES
LONDON • BOSTON • SYDNEY • AUCKLAND

Flyaway Katie

Polly Dunbar

Katie was feeling grey. She was stuck inside with no one to talk to except herself.

The picture on Katie's wall
looked a much better place to be.

So to cheer herself up,
she put on a large green hat.

But Katie still felt a little grey.

Katie put on yellow tights

and pulled them up as high
as she could reach.

Katie felt brighter.

But not bright enough.

So she put on her blue,

blue shoes.

And she put on her best pink dress.

Getting brighter!

She painted her
lips shiny, shiny red.

She painted her
face blue like her shoes.

She painted orange
stripes on her arms.

She painted the tips of
her fingers purple.

Katie stood still so the paint could dry,

and that's when she felt ...

a flittery

fluttery

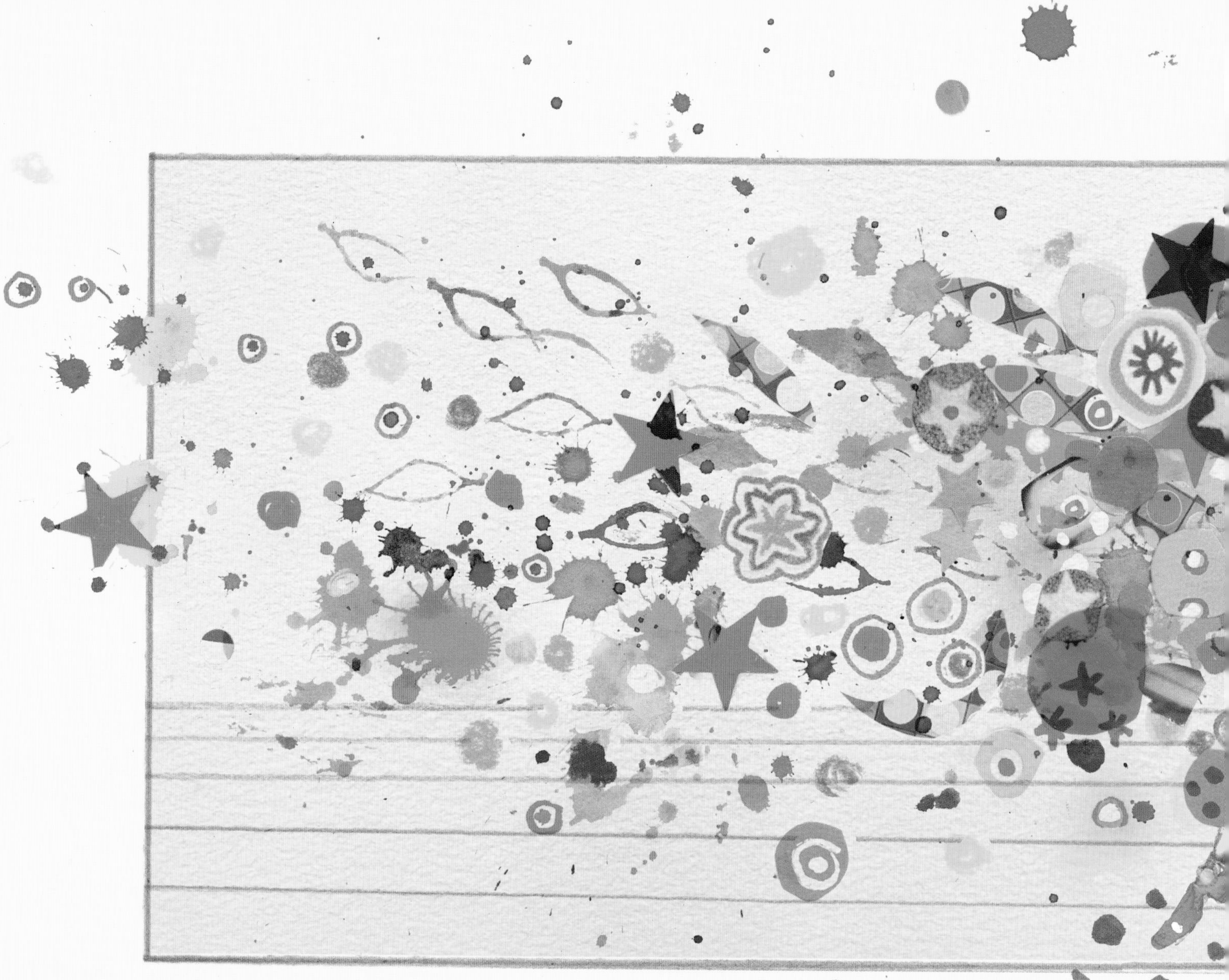

flighty

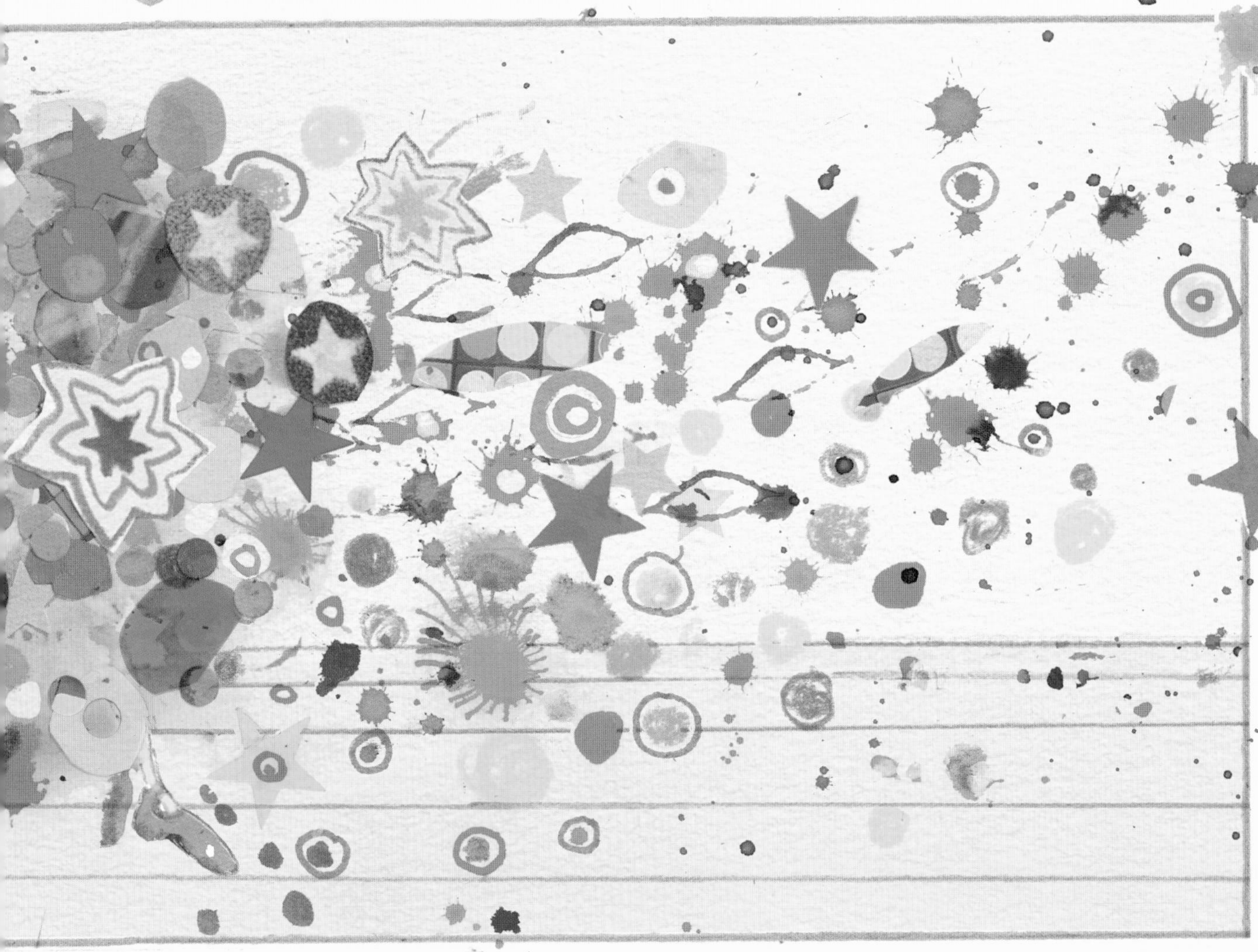

fizzling!

Whoosh!

Katie flew into the picture!

Hello, I'm Katie!
Tweet!
Tweet!
Tweet!

Tweet!
Tweet!

And that's where she stayed,
all afternoon ...

Tweet!
Tweet!

fluttering

brightly ...

until it was time to fly home ...

for her bath!

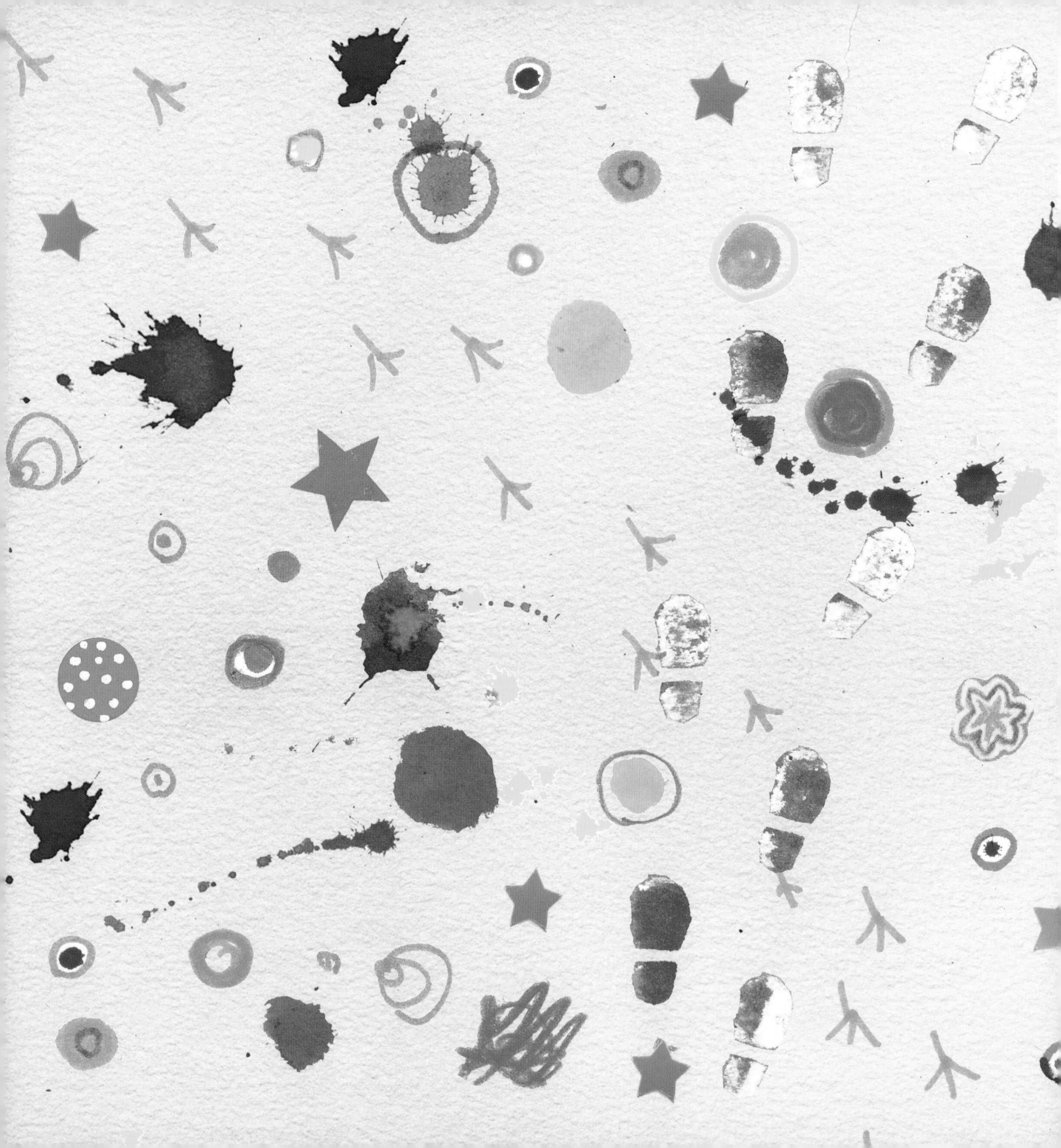

WALKER BOOKS is the world's leading independent publisher of children's books. Working with the best authors and illustrators we create books for all ages, from babies to teenagers – books your child will grow up with and always remember. So…

FOR THE BEST CHILDREN'S BOOKS,
LOOK FOR THE BEAR